Chapter One

It was the beginning of the long summer holidays but Kevin's mum still had to work all day, so he was left with his grandad, Joe.

They played games in the garden and did drawing and cutting out in the kitchen.

What do you fancy?

Bangers and mash

'Well that's all right,' said Grandad Joe. 'I like mash too. We always had mash when I was a lad. I can make that.'

So that's what they had, but his
grandad's mash wasn't like his
mother's.
It was **Lumpy**
Well, that was what Grandad liked;
lumpy mash.

But Kevin hated lumps in his food,
especially in mash. He refused to
eat it. That upset Grandad.

Kevin ran outside and slammed the door.

It wasn't until he was outside on the front doorstep that he looked at the money Grandad Joe had given him.

It wasn't a coin he'd ever seen before –

a bit larger than a ten penny piece –
and very worn and smooth.

HALF-CROWN?

He looked
closer at it.

Kevin felt very strange. Was it
trying to read the worn-down
letters that made him feel so weird?

Silly old Grandad! You couldn't spend old money like that! Kevin felt dizzy and weak at the knees.

He just had to sit down on the front step.

He looked up suddenly at the sound of a van stopping in the street.

He couldn't focus on it at first.
A sort of hazy mist made the street
look like an old faded photograph.

Then the mist cleared and he saw
that it was an old-fashioned
delivery van.

The side opened with
a clatter, dropping
to make a counter.

It's a
travelling
shop !

Now he wouldn't have
to walk all the way
to the High Street.

I don't suppose
Mum will mind

Kevin stood up, feeling quite
normal again and ran down the
steps to the van.

A lady appeared at the counter.

12

From under the counter she pulled
out a small packet. The label said
'Magic Mash.'

Kevin ran up the steps.
He didn't see the van drive away,
but after he'd opened the door,
he looked back –

and it had vanished!

Chapter Two

When Kevin got in he handed the packet of mash to Grandad.

'I've never seen this make before' said Joe.

They expected it to swell up into delicious mashed potato . . .

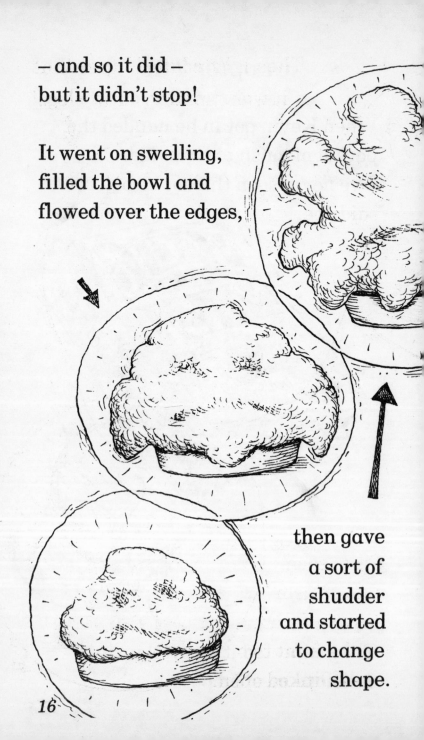

– and so it did –
but it didn't stop!

It went on swelling,
filled the bowl and
flowed over the edges,

then gave
a sort of
shudder
and started
to change
shape.

16

Then it lifted itself up so that
it was standing on two legs!

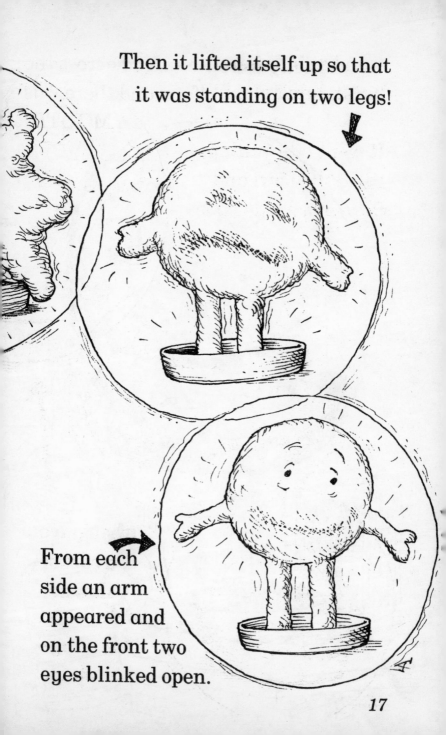

From each
side an arm
appeared and
on the front two
eyes blinked open.

Finally a crease spread across the 'face' and there was a MOUTH!

The Mash spoke, in a mashy sort
of voice:

'I . . . er . . . What? . . . um . . . It
wasn't me. It was him,' stammered
Kevin, pointing at Grandad Joe.

The Mash creature turned to
Grandad.

'Hold on, you monster mash, or
whatever you are,' said Grandad.
'Don't you go calling me names.'

'Sorry,' said the Mash, 'but I have to talk like that, it's expected. Do you want anything or not?'

'Sorry,' said the Mash.

'One day, one mix, one wish.
That's your lot!'
And with a PLOP!

. . . he disappeared
and there in front of them were two
plates of sausages and mash.

This is good, isn't it?

What a waste of a wish

When Kevin's mother came home
that evening they didn't say a word
about the Mash.

What's wrong
with him?

Grandad just sat with a smile on his
face thinking about what he could
have wished for.

Chapter Three

Next morning, when Mum had left, Grandad suggested an early dinner of burgers and beans.

'I've been thinking,' said Kevin.
'I want a really big wish today.'
So they gulped down their dinner and washed up.

Kevin spooned
out the powder.

Grandad poured on the boiling water.
'That's not enough for a really big
wish,' he said. 'Go on, put
some more in!' and
he jogged Kevin's
elbow so that
a great

dollop
of
powder
splattered
into
the
bowl.

Oh no, Grandad,
what have you
done now?

But it was too late. The mash swelled
up faster than they could stir it,

spread over
the table
and down
the sides.

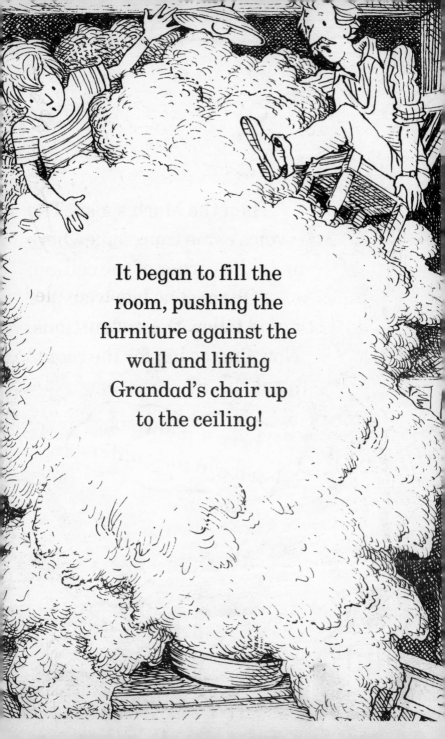

It began to fill the room, pushing the furniture against the wall and lifting Grandad's chair up to the ceiling!

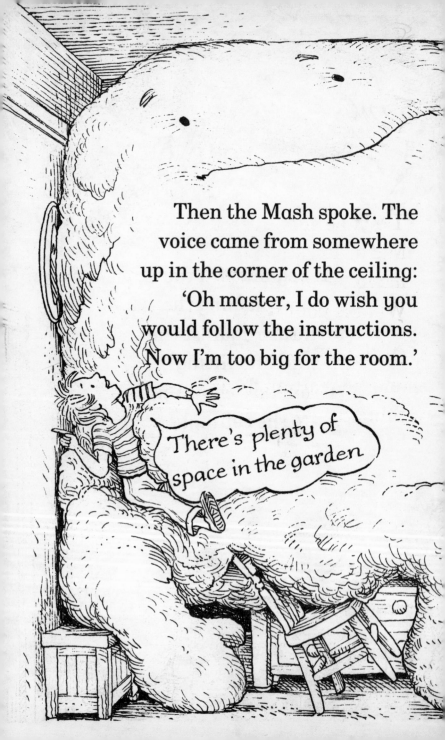

Then the Mash spoke. The voice came from somewhere up in the corner of the ceiling: 'Oh master, I do wish you would follow the instructions. Now I'm too big for the room.'

There's plenty of space in the garden

'Don't be daft,' hissed the Mash. 'I'm stuck. I can't move. Anyhow, here goes . . . What is your wish, Oh masters?'

Grandad's voice came from another corner: 'I can't think from up here.'

'What was that?' asked the Mash.

said the Mash, wriggling its
arms with some difficulty.

With a long sad hiss the Mash sank
slowly to the floor. Grandad was
gently lowered to his place by the
table before the Mash disappeared
with a . . .

'You've done it again,' grumbled Kevin. 'You've wasted another wish.' 'Well, you wouldn't want me to hurt myself, would you?' said Grandad.

'Look in the packet,' said Kevin. 'There's only a little bit left.' 'Tomorrow,' said Grandad, 'We'll think before we wish.'

Chapter Four

This time they mixed the mash properly.

Two exact tablespoons; add boiling water; and there was the Mash.

'What is your wish, Oh masters?'
'Fish and chips . . .' said Grandad.

'. . . beside the sea,' added Kevin.

'Your slightest wish. . .and all that,'
said the Mash. 'Come outside into
the garden.'

He poured himself
out of the open window
like a drift of thick fog.

They stood together in the garden.

He gathered them up
in his cloudy arms and
lifted them up above
the houses, across the
field and woods,

in a great creamy
arc as high as the
clouds and dropped
them gently on to the
grassy top of the cliff
above the beach.

'Oh silly me,' said the Mash, 'My fault. They must have thought I was a rain cloud.'

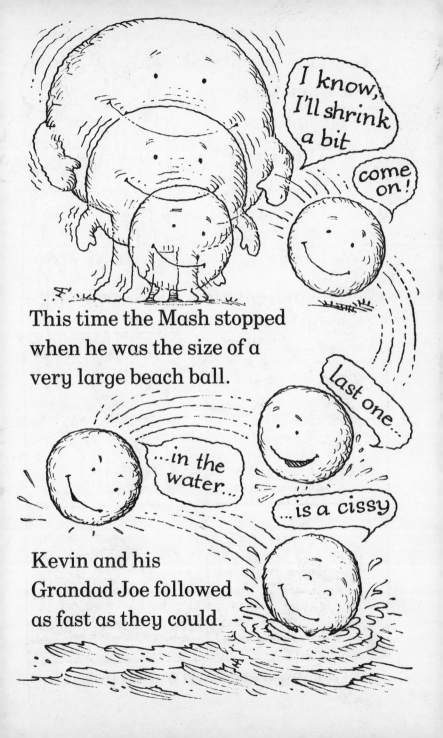

This time the Mash stopped when he was the size of a very large beach ball.

Kevin and his Grandad Joe followed as fast as they could.

Grandad was puffed out when they reached the sea.

I'm not as young as I was

So Kevin went along the beach with the Mash-ball and played . . .

until they were both puffed out.

Chapter Five

Then the bully-boys turned up.
There were three of them,
swaggering along
the beach,

kicking sand
on to picnics,

and stamping
on sandcastles.

Then they saw the big beach ball.

They gave a shout and ran to kick it.

'Bring it back!' shouted Kevin.
One of the boys turned round.

He gave Kevin
a push so that he
fell over backwards.

Then suddenly . . .

... the Mash ball bounced back and hit him.

He blamed the others for doing it.

They all started arguing, while the
ball bounced between them.

Kevin and Grandad slipped away to
a cafe near the beach.

Soon the bully boys were all
fighting and shouting at each other.

The fish and chips were delicious.
'I've never tasted better,'
said Grandad Joe.
'Nor me,' agreed Kevin as he slipped
the last chip into his mouth. Then . . .

Kevin nearly choked on the chip.

Luckily, when he went to pay for
the meal he found enough money in
his pocket to pay the bill and their
bus fares home.

Chapter Six

Grandad Joe
was rather stiff
the next morning.
'Oh dear,' he moaned.
'I'm not used to all that
running about.
I wish I was young again.'

Oh dear,
my old bones

What did you do
when you were
young Grandad?

We played
in the street.
There wasn't
so much
traffic then

We played lots of games . . .

roller-skate hockey . . . football . . . and

'kick-pot-orny' . . . and tying
door-knockers together.

Kevin went to watch
the television, leaving
Grandad, dreaming
of his young days . . .

Then Grandad did a
very selfish thing.

He used up the last
of the Magic Mash!

Chapter Seven

Grandad wandered dreamily out
of the house, hand in hand with
the genie of the mash.

'Grandad!' called
Kevin. 'What shall
we do today?'

Grandad wasn't
in the kitchen.
'Grandad, where are you?'

Kevin looked everywhere;
but he couldn't find his
Grandad. Joe
had vanished!
Kevin sat down
to think.

Then he looked
into the packet
of Magic Mash.
It was EMPTY!

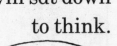

There was a knock at the front door.

Kevin opened it. There was no one
there. Perhaps it was the back door.

But no one was there either.
There was another knock. This
time, Kevin waited by the door.
He had an idea.

When the next knock came Kevin
opened the door straight away. But
not quickly enough. He saw a
strangely-dressed boy disappearing
round the street corner.

So he sat on
the doorstep
and waited.

Before long the boy
looked round the
corner. Then Kevin
knew who it was.
'All right, Joe,' called
Kevin.'I saw you.
You can come out now.'
The boy came and sat
on the step beside Kevin.

'Coming to play?' he said.
'Just for a while,' said Kevin.
'Till dinner time. But not here.'

'Why not? We always play in this street,' asked the boy.

'Too much traffic. Let's go to the park,' suggested Kevin.

They kicked a can around

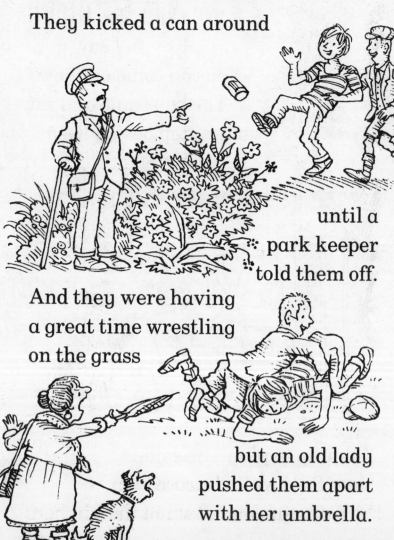

until a park keeper told them off.

And they were having a great time wrestling on the grass

but an old lady pushed them apart with her umbrella.

So they had a race back to
the house and sat down in the kitchen.

They peeled some potatoes and chopped them up. Joe put them on to boil and fried the sausages.

When the potatoes
were nearly done,
the two boys
strained them,

mashed them

and put in butter,
a drop of milk
and salt.

Kevin and young Joe enjoyed their lumpy mashed potatoes. The Magic Mash watched rather sadly from the top of the cupboard. Then he said . . .

Wait for it. Ready... NOW!

And there was Kevin with an
empty plate and sitting next to him
was Grandad Joe.

'Well, that's that,' said Kevin.
'It was fun while it lasted but that's
the end of the Magic Mash.'

Grandad Joe grinned: 'Oh, I don't know. Look what I found in young Joe's trouser pocket.'

And he held up a shining new silver HALF CROWN.